17235

A NOTE TO PARENTS

Reading Aloud with Your Child

Research shows that reading books aloud is the single most valuable support parents can provide in helping children learn to read.

- Be a ham! The more enthusiasm you display, the more your child will enjoy the book.
- Run your finger underneath the words as you read to signal that the print carries the story.
- Leave time for examining the illustrations more closely; encourage your child to find things in the pictures.
- Invite your youngster to join in whenever there's a repeated phrase in the text.
- Link up events in the book with similar events in your child's life.
- If your child asks a question, stop and answer it. The book can be a means to learning more about your child's thoughts.

Listening to Your Child Read Aloud

The support of your attention and praise is absolutely crucial to your child's continuing efforts to learn to read.

- If your child is learning to read and asks for a word, give it immediately so that the meaning of the story is not interrupted. DO NOT ask your child to sound out the word.
- On the other hand, if your child initiates the act of sounding out, don't intervene.
- If your child is reading along and makes what is called a miscue, listen for the sense of the miscue. If the word "road" is substituted for the word "street," for instance, no meaning is lost. Don't stop the reading for a correction.
- If the miscue makes no sense (for example, "horse" for "house"), ask your child to reread the sentence because you're not sure you understand what's just been read.
- Above all else, enjoy your child's growing command of print and make sure you give lots of praise. *You are your child's first teacher — and the most important one. Praise from you is critical for further risk-taking and learning.*

— Priscilla Lynch
Ph.D., New York University
Educational Consultant

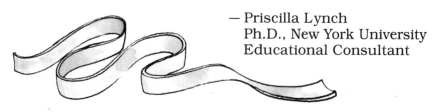

To the World Seido Karate Organization
and the many patient Senseis
— E.L.

To Granny and Pop
— D.B.

Text copyright © 1996 by Elizabeth Levy.
Illustrations copyright © 1996 by Denise Brunkus.
All rights reserved. Published by Scholastic Inc.
HELLO READER!, CARTWHEEL BOOKS, and the CARTWHEEL BOOKS logo are registered trademarks of Scholastic Inc.
The HELLO READER! logo is a trademark of Scholastic Inc.

Library of Congress Cataloging-in-Publication Data
Levy, Elizabeth.
The karate class mystery / by Elizabeth Levy ; illustrated by Denise Brunkus.
    p.   cm. — (Hello reader! Level 4) (Invisible Inc. ; #5)
    Summary: When someone takes Justin's karate belt, his friends in Invisible Inc. try to determine a motive as they investigate the mystery.
    ISBN 0-590-60323-X
    [1. Karate — Fiction.   2. Lost and found possessions — Fiction.
3. Mystery and detective stories.]
I. Brunkus, Denise, ill.   II. Title.   III. Series.   IV. Series: Levy, Elizabeth.
Invisible Inc. ; #5.
PZ7.L5827Kar   1996
[Fic]—dc20   95-50527
                                    | 72 35   CIP
                                                                          AC

12 11 10 9 8 7 6 5 4 3 2 1   6 7 8 9/9 0 1/0

                          Printed in the U.S.A.   24

                First Scholastic printing, September 1996

The
Karate Class
Mystery

by Elizabeth Levy

Illustrated by
Denise Brunkus

Hello Reader! — Level 4

SCHOLASTIC INC.

Cartwheel
·B·O·O·K·S· ®

New York Toronto London Auckland Sydney

Chip fell into a strange pool of water. Now Chip is invisible.

Justin knows how to read lips because of his hearing loss.

Charlene is sometimes bossy, but always brave.

Together they are **Invisible Inc.** — and they solve mysteries!

CHAPTER 1

Strong Spirit-
Warrior Spirit

"EEYAHHH!" yelled Charlene. She walked into Chip's yard. She kicked into the air. Her legs flew out from under her and she fell down.

"Yikes!" shouted Chip. He jumped out of the way.

"This karate stuff is harder than it looks," said Charlene, picking herself up. She showed Chip an ad for a new karate school.

"I think we need lessons," said Charlene. "Let's visit this school now."

"What about Justin?" asked Chip.

"Justin's been disappearing every afternoon," said Charlene. "Kind of like you," she joked. "Let's go to the karate school. We'll tell Justin about it later."

Chip and Charlene walked to the karate school. A man dressed in a white jacket and pants greeted them. He wore a frayed black belt with gold stripes on one end.

"We're two-thirds of Invisible Inc.," said Charlene. She gave the karate teacher an Invisible Inc. card. "We want to learn karate."

"Welcome. I'm Sensei Bobby," said the man. "Sensei means teacher." Sensei Bobby looked at Chip curiously. "How did you become invisible?" he asked.

Chip told him his story. He liked the fact that Sensei Bobby wanted to know. Most adults tried to pretend that it was no big deal.

"Well, you'll make a very interesting student," said Sensei Bobby. He

took out two new white uniforms and white belts. "The karate student wears a *gi*. Here is one for each of you. I'll write your names on them in permanent ink — not invisible ink." Sensei Bobby smiled at his joke. He wrote Chip's and Charlene's names on the jackets and the pants and in very small letters on the belts.

Sensei Bobby gave them the uniforms. "Keep your *gi* neat and clean. But never wash the belt. Every drop of sweat and hard work that you put into your training will show on your belt. It's something to be proud of. Now go change for class."

They walked into the classroom. The place was very clean. Students were quietly stretching.

"It's very quiet," said Charlene. Charlene didn't like things too quiet. She took a juice box out of her backpack.

Suddenly, one of the students turned and kicked.

"It's Justin!" shouted Charlene. She was so excited that she flung her hand in the air, and orange juice spilled on Justin's belt. "Justin, what are you doing here?"

"Oh, no," moaned Justin. "My belt!"

"It's just a little orange juice," said Charlene. "It'll wash off."

"I can't wash my belt. You don't know anything about karate," said Justin.

"That's your fault! Why didn't you tell us you were taking karate?" asked Charlene.

Justin was embarrassed. He wanted to have one part of his life that was private. He wasn't very good at sports, but he loved karate. Justin's hearing loss wasn't a problem for him in this sport. He depended on his eyes to learn how to imitate Sensei Bobby's movements. Justin was good at watching people.

One of the students bowed to Justin. "Could you help me with '*Seiken Jodan Tuski*?' I keep forgetting what it means."

"Oh, sure," said Justin. "*Seiken* means 'fist' in Japanese. *Jodan* means 'face' and *tuski* means 'punch.'"

"Oh, no!" exclaimed Charlene. "Keith Broder is here, too!" Keith Broder was a boy at school who was always giving Invisible Inc. trouble.

Keith turned to a girl who was punching the air. "Hey, Cuz, come meet Chip. He's the original airhead — because his face is air."

"Keith Broder, you shouldn't call Chip an airhead," said Charlene.

"I agree," said the girl. "My cousin, Keith, has a lot of air in his head — hot air. I'm Tonya Sharlip. I just moved here." Tonya looked at

Justin who was fussing with his belt.

"This is my lucky belt," mumbled Justin. "I've had it since my first day. I became powerful the first day I put this belt on."

Sensei Bobby clapped his hands. "Line up! Class, I'd like you to welcome our new students, Chip and

Charlene. The two of you can stand behind Justin. He knows the moves very well. Justin, introduce yourself."

"Uh, they know me," said Justin. "I'm part of Invisible Inc."

"You could have fooled me," said Charlene. She still felt angry because Justin had kept a secret from her.

"What's Invisible Inc.?" asked Tonya.

"We're detectives," said Charlene proudly. "One of the rules for Invisible Inc. is that we stick together. Right, Justin?"

Justin rolled his eyes.

"How do you join Invisible Inc.?" asked Tonya. "It sounds like fun."

"It isn't just for fun," said Charlene in her bossy way. "You have to be very good at solving mysteries. And once we all learn karate, we'll be even better."

"Charlene and Tonya," said Sensei Bobby gently, "in karate, students do not talk in class. Our dojo, or training hall, is a special place where we show courtesy to each other. First you learn to bow to show respect. When you bow, you say, '*Osu*.' It means 'hello' and 'goodbye.' It also means, 'I understand. I'll try my best.'"

Sensei Bobby showed some punches. "Punch the air in front of you and shout *'Kiai'* with strong spirit. I want 'Bushido Spirit,' the spirit of warriors."

Punching the air was hard work. Soon everybody was sweating.

Afterward Charlene went up to Justin. "Karate is fun," she said. "And you're really good."

"Thanks. I'm sorry I kept it a secret. I have a good book on karate that will help you learn faster."

"*Osu!*" said Charlene, bowing the way she had learned in class.

Justin dug into his backpack and pulled out his book. Just as he was giving it to Charlene, Sensei Bobby called him over. Justin left his backpack on the floor.

"Justin," said Sensei Bobby, "I think you will be ready for promotion from white belt to yellow belt next Saturday."

This is my chance, Charlene said to herself as she took Justin's belt out of his backpack. But she didn't know that she was being watched by an invisible boy.

Charlene walked quickly into the
girls' locker room.

"Oh, hi, Tonya," she said.

CHAPTER 2

The End of Invisible Inc.?

The next day, as Justin was putting on his *gi*, he couldn't find his belt. Chip helped him look for it all around the locker room.

"I never take it out of my backpack," said Justin.

Chip had a sick feeling. He knew how mad Charlene had been at Justin for not telling them he was taking karate.

When they went out on the dojo floor, Justin ran up to Charlene. "I've got a customer for Invisible Inc."

Charlene looked excited. "Who? We'll be so good, now that we know karate."

"Me," said Justin. "Somebody

stole my belt."

Charlene made a face. "That's not much of a mystery. Maybe you left it at home." Chip gave Charlene a funny look, but of course, she couldn't tell. Nobody could tell when Chip made a face.

"I've put a lot of sweat into my belt," said Justin. "I'd like to clobber whoever took it."

"Justin," said Sensei Bobby, who was about to start class, "you of all people know that karate isn't just about fighting. I don't like that kind of talk in the dojo. Remember the dojo rules. No taunts. No put-downs. What is the problem?"

"My belt is gone!" said Justin.

"Your belt is very important," said Sensei Bobby. "You were supposed to take care of it."

"I know," said Justin. "I've had

that belt since my very first karate class."

"I can give you another one," said Sensei Bobby. "But, please return it when you find your belt."

Justin put on the new belt, but it didn't feel right. Twice during class it came untied. Justin had to kneel down and retie it. The third time it happened, Sensei Bobby became impatient. During *kata*, a combination of movements, punches, and blocks, Justin kept turning in the wrong direction. Normally, he could do his *kata* without thinking.

Nothing went right for Justin all during practice. Finally, after class, Chip said, "I'm calling a meeting of Invisible Inc. Charlene, please come here now."

"You promised to come to my house," said Tonya to Charlene.

"Yeah, I did," said Charlene. "Chip, let's meet tomorrow. Okay?"

"Not okay," said Chip. "Justin, I've got something to tell you. That's why Invisible Inc. has to meet today."

"Oh, just say what you want to

say," said Charlene, bossily. "Tonya and I want to practice our *kata*."

"All right, Charlene," said Chip. "I was trying to keep this private, but you want it out in the open. Tell Justin why you took his belt."

"Why I did what?" shouted Charlene.

"Why she did what?" said Justin.

"Yesterday, after class, I saw you," said Chip. "You took Justin's belt."

"Oh, Charlene," said Justin sadly. "Why would you do that?"

"I didn't take it," said Charlene.

"I saw you take it into the girls' locker room," said Chip.

"I tried to wipe off the orange juice I spilled on it," explained Charlene. "Then I put it back in Justin's backpack. Tonya was there. Don't you remember, Tonya?"

"I remember that you had it in the locker room," said Tonya, "but I didn't see you return it."

"I didn't take it. Honest," said Charlene.

But no one seemed to believe her. Was this the end of Invisible Inc.?

CHAPTER 3

Visible Inc.

Before he lost his belt, Justin was the best karate student in his class. Now Justin felt as if he were the worst.

"Everybody down on the floor," said Sensei Bobby on Friday. "Push-ups. Justin, count off."

Justin started to count in Japanese, "*Ichi, Ni, San, Shi, Go* [1,2,3,4,5]." Suddenly his mind went blank. He couldn't remember what came after five.

"Uh. *Hachi*," said Justin.

"*Hachi* is eight. *Roku* is six," said Sensei Bobby. "Justin, you should know that."

Justin felt terrible. Usually he knew how to count in Japanese. *It's this stupid belt*, he thought. *I need*

*my real belt. Everything's gone
wrong since I lost it.*

After class, Justin went over to
Charlene. "If you hadn't taken my
belt, I wouldn't be having so many
problems," he said.

"I didn't take your belt," said Charlene.

"Charlene," said Chip, "you have to tell the truth."

"I *am* telling the truth!" cried Charlene.

Chip and Justin shook their heads. They walked out of the karate school together.

"Bummer," Tonya said to Charlene. "I thought you said that Invisible Inc. stuck together."

"What am I going to do?" said Charlene. "Invisible Inc. is falling apart."

"Maybe you should join Visible Inc.," said Tonya.

"What's that?" asked Charlene.

"You and me," said Tonya. "I believe you didn't take Justin's belt. You and I could find out who did it."

Charlene clapped her hands

together. "Then we'll march that person right up to Justin and Chip — and won't they be sorry!"

"You bet," said Tonya. "Okay. How do we start?"

"Usually, Chip goes invisible," said Charlene. "But we can't do that. So we have to use our brains. First we have to think about why someone would steal Justin's belt. Maybe someone is jealous and doesn't want Justin to get a promotion! Or maybe someone lost his or her own belt and is afraid to tell Sensei Bobby, so that person took Justin's belt. Now, who could it be?"

Tonya made a face. "Keith is my cousin, so maybe I shouldn't say this. But Justin is much better than Keith at karate, even though they started at the same time."

"We need to get a look at Keith's belt," said Charlene. "But how? He's gone home."

"I can get into Keith's house," said Tonya.

Charlene and Tonya went to Keith's house. Keith was practicing karate on his front porch. His father was watching him. "I want to go for my promotion at the same time Justin does," said Keith. "So I'm practicing my *kata*."

"How are we going to get him to take the belt off?" whispered Charlene.

"Watch me," said Tonya.

Tonya started to hold her nose. "Wow, Keith, your uniform stinks."

"Tonya's right," said his father. "Keith, I've got to do some laundry anyway. Give me your uniform. I'll wash it."

Keith rolled his eyes, but went upstairs to change. Tonya knocked on his door. "Give it to me. I'll bring it down to your dad," said Tonya. She giggled at Charlene.

"Okay," said Keith, handing her his uniform. "But give me my belt back. That doesn't get washed."

Keith grabbed the belt — but not before Tonya saw Keith's name on it.

"Keith doesn't have Justin's belt," she said to Charlene.

Charlene was sad. She missed Justin and Chip. Visible Inc. just wasn't as much fun as Invisible Inc.

CHAPTER 4

Motive-Shmotive!

"I've got another great idea," said Tonya when she and Charlene were outside Keith's house. "What about Chip?"

"Chip!" exclaimed Charlene. "He would never take Justin's belt. He and Justin are best friends. Chip doesn't have a motive."

"Motive-shmotive!" scoffed Tonya. "He has the opportunity. He can go invisible any time. Chip's the one who accused you in the first place. Maybe he blamed you because he doesn't want anyone to know that he really did it."

"It doesn't sound like Chip," said Charlene.

"You can't trust anyone if you want to be a detective," said Tonya.

"You've got to be hard-nosed. Let's go to Chip's house now and look at his belt."

And Justin and Chip think that I'm bossy, Charlene said to herself as she followed Tonya over to Chip's house.

Justin was trying to show Chip how to do the *kata*. "You've got to look and then pivot," said Justin.

Tonya sniffed and held her nose. "Chip, you're supposed to keep your *gi* clean. You'd better put it in the laundry." Tonya was hoping to play the same trick on Chip as she had played on Keith.

"You should have your nose checked," said Chip. "I just washed my *gi*."

Justin made a face. "Let's keep practicing. I'm never going to get my promotion the way things have been going."

"Justin, I know you're going to get your promotion," said Charlene. "You're really good."

"Not without my lucky belt," said Justin.

Suddenly Tonya shrieked. "Help!" Something was pulling her shoelace.

Chip laughed. "It's just my dog, Max. He likes to pull on shoelaces and belts."

"He's weird," said Tonya.

"He's invisible except for his tail," said Charlene. Max had given her an idea for getting Chip's belt.

"Could I practice *kata* with you?" Charlene asked Chip and Justin.

"Well, Sensei Bobby said we should help each other," said Chip.

Chip knelt down and gave Charlene the end of his belt for a leg stretch.

But Charlene dangled the belt in front of Max. Her idea worked. Max grabbed Chip's belt and ran away with it.

"Sorry," Charlene said to Chip as she ran after Max.

Charlene was out of breath when she finally caught the belt. She eagerly read the name: Chip. Another bad guess!

Suddenly, Charlene thought she knew who really took Justin's belt. But how could she prove it?

CHAPTER 5

Invisible Boy in the Girls' Locker Room

It was Monday, the day Justin would take his test for promotion. Everybody at the dojo was excited.

Nobody was more nervous than Chip. And he wasn't even up for promotion. Chip stood outside the girls' locker room in the dojo.

"Go on, Chip. You've got to do it. It's empty. I checked," said Charlene. "Don't you want to help me clear my name?"

"Yes ... but why can't *you* do it?" asked Chip.

"Because she could walk in and see me and catch me looking at her things!" explained Charlene. "I'll just wait outside and make sure no

one goes in."

"Sometimes I wish you were invisible instead of me," said Chip. He was so embarrassed. Charlene thought she saw pink where Chip's face would be.

A few minutes later, Chip came

back out. "It's not there," he said.

"Did you look where I told you?" insisted Charlene.

"I looked everywhere," said Chip. "I didn't find Justin's belt. The only belt I saw in there had Tonya's name on it."

Charlene sighed. Justin came by, looking worried. "No luck?" he asked.

"Not yet," said Charlene. "Did you take the written part of the test?"

Justin nodded. "I could remember most of the Japanese words, but I'll never pass the next part."

"Just think 'strong spirit,'" said Charlene.

Sensei Bobby came out of his office. Charlene and Justin bowed.

"Come, Justin," said Sensei Bobby. "It's time for your test on your strength and *kata*."

Justin bowed to Sensei Bobby
again.

Just then, Tonya walked in from
the street dressed in her uniform.
Charlene rushed over to her. "I
thought you left your uniform in your
cubby."

"I did," said Tonya. "But after smelling Keith's *gi*, I thought I should wash mine, too!"

"You didn't wash the belt. Did you?" asked Charlene.

"Of course not," said Tonya.

"Shh," said Chip. "Look at Justin."

Justin was doing push-ups. Sensei Bobby put his hand on Justin's back, just to make it harder. But Justin was strong.

Then Sensei Bobby stood in front of Justin. "I want you to close your eyes and do *kata* number one."

Justin's eyes got round. "But, but . . . if I close my eyes, I can't read your lips," he said. "I can't hear well. I won't know where the other people are. And I don't have my real belt — the one I put so much sweat into."

"You can do it!" said Sensei Bobby. "Concentrate."

Justin's heart beat very fast. He took a deep breath and closed his eyes.

Justin moved to the left, blocked, stepped forward, and punched the air. Then came the trickiest part. He

had to do many turns. He finished his *kata* with a loud "KIAAA!"

Sensei Bobby tapped Justin on the shoulder and said, "*Yame!* Open your eyes."

Sensei Bobby bowed to Justin. Justin bowed back.

"You did very well," said Sensei Bobby with a little smile. "You are finished."

Justin went over to his friends. "I think I passed," he said.

"And I know where your belt is," said Charlene. "Tonya, you're wearing a belt that has orange spots on it! That's Justin's belt."

"You think *I* stole it?" said Tonya. "But I'm your partner."

"No, Chip and Justin are my partners," said Charlene. "You took Justin's belt and then you just pre-

tended to look for it with me.

"Chip saw me take it," continued
Charlene. "But then I put it back.
I tried to get the orange spots out.
But I couldn't. Tonya saw me. She
must have taken the belt out after I
put it back."

"I'm sorry," said Tonya. "Justin said that his belt gave him power. He's so much better at karate than I am. I thought that his lucky belt would make me better. Also, I felt left out, because you were all detectives. And then it was so much fun being a detective with you, Charlene."

"It wasn't Justin's belt that gave him the power," said Chip. "It was all the hard work he does. If we do that hard work, we're going to get our promotions, too."

"Chip's right, Tonya," said Justin. "You can keep my belt. I'm going to get a yellow belt. Maybe someday I'll get a black belt. Maybe someday you'll be a detective. But not yet! You've got a lot to learn."

Justin put his arms around Charlene and Chip. "Karate is a lot like being a good detective — it's hard work and strong spirit."

"KIAAA!" shouted the three detectives from Invisible Inc.

Sensei Bobby bowed in their direction. "I like that Bushido Spirit."

"It's the spirit of Invisible Inc.," said Charlene.

"Nothing can keep us apart," said Justin. "Not even a missing belt."